# The Zookeeper's Sleepers

Written by Frank B. Edwards
Illustrated by John Bianchi

star

ZOOKEEPER

house

path

I am awake. I cannot sleep.

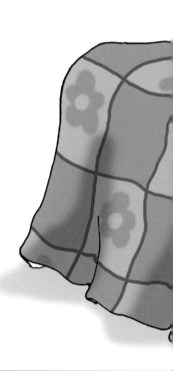

Take this book and
read a bedtime story.

We are awake. We cannot sleep.

Take these books and
read a bedtime story.

We are awake.
We cannot sleep.

Take these books and
read a bedtime story.

We are awake.
We cannot sleep.

Take these books and
read a bedtime story.

Come here and I will read to you.

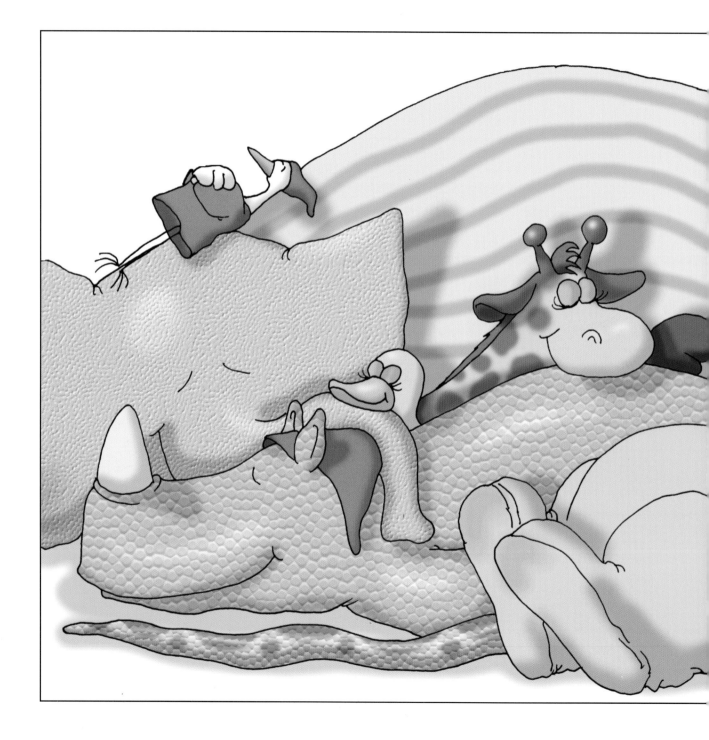

Now I am awake and I cannot sleep.

The End